STORM-BOY

STORM-BOY

STORY BY
Colin Thiele
DRAWINGS BY
Robert Ingpen

NEW
HOLLAND

Also by Colin Thiele:

Children's Books
Rim of the Morning
Klontarf
Pinquo
Stories Short and Tall
The Sun on the Stubble
February Dragon
Mrs Munch and Puffing Billy
Blue Fin
Flash Flood
Flip Flop and Tiger Snake
Gloop the Bunyip
The Fire in the Stone
Albatross Two
Magpie Island
Uncle Gustav's Ghosts
The Hammerhead Light
The Shadow on the Hills
The Sknuks
River Murray Mary
Ballander Boy (*with David Simpson*)
Tanya and Trixie (*with David Simpson*)
The Valley Between
Little Tom Little (*with David Simpson*)
The Undercover Secret

Educational
The State of Our State
Looking at Poetry
Handbook to Favourite Australian Stories
Grains of Mustard Seed

Verse
Man in a Landscape
In Charcoal and Conte
Selected Verse
Songs for My Thongs

General
Heysen of Hahndorf
Barossa Valley Sketchbook
Labourers in the Vineyard
Coorong
Range Without Man
The Little Desert
The Bight
Heysen's Early Hahndorf
Lincoln's Place
Maneater Man

Also by Robert Ingpen:

Pioneers of Wool
Pioneer Settlement in Australia
Robe: A Portrait of the Past
The Runaway Punt (*with Michael Page*)
Turning Points in the History of Australia (*with Michael Page*)
Lincoln's Place (*with Colin Thiele*)
Paradise and Beyond (*with Nick Evers*)

Published in Australia by
New Holland Publishers (Australia) Pty Ltd
Sydney • Auckland • London • Cape Town

14 Aquatic Drive Frenchs Forest NSW 2086 Australia
218 Lake Road Northcote Auckland New Zealand
86 Edgware Road London W2 2EA United Kingdom
80 McKenzie Street Cape Town 8001 South Africa

This edition first published in hardback by Rigby Publishers 1974
Reprinted 1975, 1978, 1979, 1980
Reprinted by Weldon Publishing 1990, 1992
Reprinted in paperback by Lansdowne Publishing Pty Ltd 1995, 1997
Reprinted by New Holland Publishers (Australia) Pty Ltd 2004

10 9 8 7 6 5 4 3 2 1

A CiP record of this title is available from the National Library of Australia

Printed in China by Everbest Printing Co. Ltd

Storm-boy lived between the Coorong and the sea. His home was the long, long snout of sandhill and scrub that curves away south-eastwards from the Murray Mouth. A wild strip it is, windswept and tussocky, with the flat shallow water of the South Australian Coorong on one side and the endless slam of the Southern Ocean on the other. They call it the Ninety Mile Beach. From thousands of miles round the cold, wet underbelly of the world the waves come sweeping in towards the shore and pitch down in a terrible ruin of white water and spray. All day and all night they tumble and thunder. And when the wind rises it whips the sand up the beach and the white spray darts and writhes in the air like snakes of salt.

Robert Ingpen '74

Storm-Boy lived with Hide-Away Tom, his father. Their home was a rough little humpy made of wood and brush and flattened sheets of iron from old tins. It had a dirt floor, two blurry bits of glass for windows, and a little crooked chimney made of stove-pipes and wire. It was hot in summer and cold in winter, and it shivered when the great storms bent the sedges and shrieked through the bushes outside. But Storm-Boy was happy there.

Hide-Away was a quiet, lonely man. Years before, when Storm-Boy's mother had died, he had left Adelaide and gone to live like a hermit by the sea. People looked down their noses when they heard about it, and called him a beachcomber. They said it was a bad thing to take a four-year-old boy to such a wild, lonely place. But Storm-Boy and his father didn't mind. They were both happy.

People seldom saw Hide-Away or Storm-Boy. Now and then they sailed up the Coorong in their little boat, past the strange wild inlet of the Murray Mouth, past the islands and the reedy fringes of the fresh-water shore, past the pelicans and ibises and tall white cranes, to the little town with a name like a water-bird's cry—Goolwa! There Storm-Boy's father bought boxes and tins of food, coils of rope and fishing lines, new shirts and sandals, kerosene for the lamp, and lots of other packages and parcels until the little boat was loaded like a junk.

People in the street looked at them wonderingly and nudged each other. "There's Tom," they'd say, "the beach-comber from down the coast. He's come out of his hide-away for a change." And so, by and by, they just nick-named him "Hide-Away," and nobody even remembered his real name.

Storm-Boy got his name in a different way. One day some campers came through the scrub to the far side of the Coorong. They carried a boat down to the water and crossed over to the ocean beach. But a dark storm came towering in from the west during the day, heaving and boiling over Kangaroo Island and Cape Jervis, past Granite Island, the Bluff, and Port Elliot, until it swept down towards them with lightning and black rain. The campers ran back over the sandhills through the flying cloud and the gloom. Suddenly one of them stopped and pointed through a break in the rain and mist.

"Great Scot! Look! Look!"

A boy was wandering down the beach all alone. He was as calm and happy as you please, stopping every now and then to pick up shells or talk to a molly-hawk standing forlornly on the wet sand with his wings folded and his head pointing into the rising wind.

"He must be lost!" cried the camper. "Quick, take my things down to the boat; I'll run and rescue him." But when he turned round the boy had gone. They couldn't find him anywhere. The campers rushed off through the storm and raised an alarm as soon as they could get back to town:

"Quick, there's a little boy lost way down the beach," they cried. "Hurry, or we'll be too late to save him." But the postmaster at Goolwa smiled. "No need to worry," he said. "That's Hide-Away's little chap. He's your boy in the storm."

And from then on everyone called him Storm-Boy.

The only other man who lived anywhere near them was Fingerbone Bill, the Aboriginal. He was a wiry, wizened man with a flash of white teeth and a jolly black face as screwed-up and wrinkled as an old boot. He had a humpy by the shore of the Coorong about a mile away.

Fingerbone knew more about things than anyone Storm-

Boy had ever known. He could point out fish in the water and birds in the sky when even Hide-Away couldn't see a thing. He knew all the signs of wind and weather in the clouds and the sea. And he could read all the strange writing on the sandhills and beaches—the scribbly stories made by beetles and mice and bandicoots and ant-eaters and crabs and birds' toes and mysterious sliding bellies in the night. Before long Storm-Boy had learnt enough to fill a hundred books.

In his humpy Fingerbone kept a disorganised collection of iron hooks, wire netting, driftwood, leather, bits of brass, boat-oars, tins, rope, torn shirts, and an old blunderbuss. He was very proud of the blunderbuss because it still worked. It was a muzzle-loader. Fingerbone would put a charge of gun-powder into it; then he'd ram anything at all down the barrel and fix it there with a wad. Once he found a big glass marble and blew it clean through a wooden box just to prove that the blunderbuss worked. But the only time Storm-Boy ever saw Fingerbone kill anything with it was when a tiger-snake came sliding through the grass to the shore like a thin stream of black glass barred with red hot coals. As it slid over the water towards his boat Fingerbone grabbed his blunderbuss and blew the snake to pieces.

"Number One bad fellow, tiger snake," he said. "Kill him dead!" Storm-Boy never forgot. For days afterwards every stick he saw melted slowly into black glass and slid away.

At first, Hide-Away was afraid that Storm-Boy would get lost. The shore stretched on and on for ninety miles, with every sandhill and bush and tussock like the last one, so that a boy who hadn't learnt to read the beach carefully

might wander up and down for hours without finding the spot that led back home. And so Hide-Away looked for a landmark.

One day he found a big piece of timber lying with the driftwood on the beach. It had been swept from the deck of a passing ship, and it was nearly as thick and strong as the pile of a jetty. Hide-Away and Fingerbone dragged it slowly to the top of the sandhill near the humpy. There Hide-Away cut some notches in the wood for steps, and fixed a small cross-piece to it. Then they dug a deep hole, stood the pole upright in it, and stamped it down firmly.

"There," said Hide-Away. "Now you'll always have a Look-Out Post. You'll be able to see it far up the beach, and you won't get lost."

As the years went by. Storm-Boy learnt many things. All living creatures were his friends—all, that is, except the long, narrow fellows who poured themselves through the sand and sedge like glass.

In a hole at the end of a burrow under a grassy tussock he found the Fairy Penguin looking shyly at two white eggs. And when the two chicks hatched out they were little bundles of dark down as soft as dusk.

"Hullo, Mrs Penguin," said Storm-Boy each day. "How are your bits of thistle-down today?"

Fairy Penguin didn't mind Storm-Boy. Instead of pecking and hissing at him she sat back sedately on her tail and looked at him gently with mild eyes.

Sometimes in the hollows behind the sandhills where the wind had been scooping and sifting, Storm-Boy found long, white heaps of sea-shell and bits of stone, ancient mussels and cockles with curves and whorls and sharp broken edges.

"An old midden," said Hide-Away, "left by the Aborigines."

"What's a midden?"

"A camping place where they used to crack their shellfish." Fingerbone stood for a long time gazing at the great heaps of shells, as if far off in thought.

"Dark people eat, make camp, long time ago," he said a little sadly. "No whitefellow here den. For hundreds and hundreds of years, only blackfellows."

Storm-Boy looked at the big heaps of shell and wondered how long ago it must have been. He could paint it in his mind . . . the red camp-fires by the Coorong, the piccaninnies, the songs, the clicking of empty shells falling on the piles as they were thrown away. And, he thought to himself, "If that time were now, I'd be a little black boy."

But his father's voice roused him and he ran down to the beach to help dig up a bagful of big cockles for their own tea. And when they had enough for themselves they filled more bags to take up to Goolwa, because there the fishermen and the tourists were eager to pay Hide-Away money for fresh bait.

Storm-Boy stood bent over like a horse-shoe, as if he were playing leap-frog; his fingers scooped and scraped in the sand, and the salt sea slid forwards and backwards under his nose. He liked the smell and the long smooth swish of it. He was very happy.

Storm-Boy liked best of all to wander along the beach after what Hide-Away called a Big Blow. For then all kinds of treasure had been thrown up by the wind and the wild waves. There, where the wide stretch of beach was shining and swishing with the backward wash, he would

see the sea-things lying as if they'd been dropped on a sheet of glass—all kinds of weed and coloured kelp, frosty white cuttlefish, sea-urchins and star-fish, little dead sea-horses as stiff as starch, and dozens of different shells—helmets, mitres, spindles and dove-shells, whelks with purple edges, ribbed and spiral clusterwinks, murex bristling out their frills of blunt spines, nautilus as frail as frozen foam, and sometimes even a new cowry, gleaming and polished, with its underside as smooth and pink as tinted porcelain.

In places the sand would be rucked and puckered into hard smooth ripples like scales. Storm-Boy liked to scuff them with his bare soles as he walked, or balance on their cool curves with the balls of his feet.

He grew up to be supple and hardy. Most of the year he wore nothing but shorts, a shirt, and a battered old Tom Sawyer hat. But when the winter wind came sweeping up from Antarctica with ice on its tongue, licking and smoothing his cheeks into cold flat pebbles, he put on one of his father's thick coats that came down to his ankles. Then he would turn up the collar, let his hands dangle down to get lost in the huge pockets, and go outside again as snug as a penguin in a burrow. For he couldn't bear to be inside. He loved the whip of the wind too much, and the salty sting of the spray on his cheek like a slap across the face, and the endless hiss of the dying ripples at his feet.

For Storm-Boy was a storm boy.

Some distance from the place where Hide-Away and Fingerbone had built their humpies, the whole stretch of the Coorong and the land around it had been turned into a sanctuary. No one was allowed to hurt the birds there. No shooters were allowed, no hunters with decoys or nets or wire traps, not even a dog.

And so the water and the shores rippled and flapped with wings. In the early morning the tall birds stood up and clapped and cheered the rising sun. Everywhere there was the sound of bathing—a happy splashing and sousing and swishing. It sounded as if the water had been turned into a bathroom five miles long, with thousands of busy fellows gargling and gurgling and blowing bubbles together. Some were above the water, some were on it, and some were under it; a few were half on it and half under. Some were just diving into it and some just climbing out of it. Some who wanted to fly were starting to take off, running across the water with big flat feet, flapping their wings furiously, and pedalling with all their might. Some were coming in to land, with their wings braking hard and their big webbed feet splayed out ready to ski over the water as soon as they landed.

Everywhere there were criss-crossing wakes of ripples and waves and splashes. Storm-Boy felt the excitement and wonder of it; he often sat on the shore all day with his knees up and his chin cupped in his hands. Sometimes he wished he'd been born an ibis or a pelican.

BUT SOMETIMES STORM-BOY saw things that made him sad. In spite of the warnings and notices, people hurt the birds. In the open season, shooters came chasing wounded ducks up the Coorong; some sneaked into the sanctuary during the night, shot the birds at daybreak, and crept out again quickly and secretly. Visitors went trampling about, kicking the nests and breaking the eggs. And some men with rifles, who called themselves *sportsmen,* when unable to find anything else to shoot at, bet one another that they could hit an egret or a moor-hen or a heron standing innocently by the shore. And so they used the birds for target practice. And when they hit one they laughed and said, "Good shot!" and then walked off leaving it lying dead with the wind ruffling its feathers. Sometimes, if it wasn't too far away, they walked up to it, turned it over with their feet and then just left it lying there on its back.

When Storm-Boy ran back to tell his father about it, Hide-Away muttered angrily, and Fingerbone slapped his loaded blunderbuss and said, "By yimminy, I fill him with salt next time! If dem fellows come back, *boom,* I put salt on their tails."

When Storm-Boy laughed at that, Fingerbone flashed his white teeth and winked at Hide-Away. Neither of them liked seeing Storm-Boy looking sad.

When Storm-Boy went walking along the beach, or over the sandhills, or in the sanctuary, the birds were not afraid. They knew he was a friend. The pelicans sat in a row, like a lot of important old men with their heavy paunches sagging, and rattled their beaks drily in greeting; the moor-hens fussed and chattered; the ibises cut the air into strips as they jerked their curved beaks up and down; and the blue crane stood in silent dignity like a tall thin statue as Storm-Boy went past.

But one morning Storm-Boy found everything in uproar and confusion. Three or four young men had gone into the sanctuary. They had found some pelican nests—wide, rough nests of sticks, grass, and pelican feathers as big as turkey quills—and they had killed two of the big birds nesting there. After that they had scattered everything wildly with their boots, kicking and shouting and picking up the white eggs and throwing them about until they were all broken. Then they had gone off laughing.

Storm-Boy crept forward in fear and anger. From behind a tussock he looked round sadly at the ruin and

destruction. Then, just as he was about to run back to tell Fingerbone to fill his blunderbuss with salt, he heard a faint rustling and crying, and there under the sticks and grass of the broken nests were three tiny pelicans—still alive. Storm-Boy picked them up carefully and hurried back to Hide-Away with them.

Two of the baby pelicans were fairly strong, but the third was desperately sick. He was bruised and hurt and helpless. He was so weak that he couldn't even hold up his head to be fed; he just let it drop back flat on the ground as soon as Storm-Boy or Hide-Away let go of it.

"I don't think he'll live," said Hide-Away. "He's too small and sick."

Even old Fingerbone shook his head. "Dem bad fellows kill big pelican. Don't think little fellow stay alive now."

"He mustn't die," Storm-Boy said desperately. "He mustn't! He mustn't!"

He wrapped up the tiny bruised body in one of Hide-Away's scarves, and put it by the fire. All day long he watched it lying there, sometimes moving feebly or opening its beak to give a noiseless little cry. Every now and then he poured out a drop of cod-liver oil from the bottle that Hide-Away had once bought for him, and tried to trickle it down the baby bird's throat.

Night came on, and still Storm-Boy watched the sick little fellow hour after hour, until Hide-Away spoke firmly about bed and sleep. But Storm-Boy couldn't sleep. Again and again through the night he slipped out of bed and tip-toed across the dirt floor to the fireplace to make sure the baby pelican was warm enough.

And in the morning it was still living.

It was three days before the baby pelican was well

28

enough to sit up and ask for food. By then his two brothers had their beaks open hungrily all the time, although of course they were still too young to have their creels or fishing baskets ready.

"Anyone would think that I was Grandfather Pelican," said Hide-Away, "by the way they always turn to me for food."

"You'll have to be," Storm-Boy told him, "because their own father and mother are dead."

"Well, they needn't think I can spend all my time catching fish for them. Look at that fellow sitting up as if he owns the place."

"Oh, that's Mr Proud," said Storm-Boy.

"How do you do, Mr Proud." Hide-Away bowed and scratched the top of the pelican's head. "And what's your brother's name?"

"That's Mr Ponder," Storm-Boy said. "He's very wise and serious."

"And what about the tiny fellow?" asked Hide-Away. "Is he Mr Peep?"

"No, he's Mr Percival." Storm-Boy picked up the bird gently in the scarf and held him on his lap. "He's been very sick."

"Welcome," said Hide-Away. "And now Grandfather Pelican had better go and catch some fish or there won't be any tea for the three Mr P's." And he went off down to his boat.

And that was how Mr Proud, Mr Ponder, and Mr Percival came to live with Storm-Boy.

BEFORE LONG THE THREE PELICANS were big and strong. Their white necks curved up cleanly, their creels grew, and their upper beaks shone like pink pearl-shell. Every morning they spread their great white wings with the bold black edges and flew three or four times round the humpy and the beach near by to make sure that everything was in order for the new day. By then they thought it was time for breakfast, so they landed heavily beside the humpy, took a few dignified steps forward, and lined up at the back door. If Hide-Away and Storm-Boy were still in bed, the three birds stood politely for a little while waiting for some sign of movement or greeting. But if nothing happened Mr Proud and Mr Ponder began to get impatient

30

after five or ten minutes and started rattling their beaks in disapproval—a snippery-snappery, snickery-snackery sort of sound like dry reeds crackling—until someone woke up.

"All right! All right!" Storm-Boy would say sleepily. "I can hear you, Mr Proud!"

He would sit up and look at the three gentlemen standing there on parade.

"I know what you're thinking, Mr Ponder. Time for respectable people to be up."

"Time for respectable pelicans to get their *own* breakfast," Hide-Away grumbled, "instead of begging from their friends."

And as time went on, he really meant what he said.

At last Hide-Away spoke sternly to Storm-Boy.

"Mr Proud, Mr Ponder, and Mr Percival will have to go back to the sanctuary where they came from. We just can't afford to feed them any more."

Storm-Boy was sad but he always knew when his father had made up his mind. "Yes, Dad," he said.

"We'll put them in the big fish-baskets," said Hide-Away, "and take them in the boat."

"Yes, Dad," said Storm-Boy, hanging his head.

So they caught Mr Proud first, and then Mr Ponder, held their wings against their sides, and put them firmly in the fish-baskets. Neither Mr Proud nor Mr Ponder thought much of the idea. They snackered noisily at Hide-Away, raked their ruffled feathers crossly, and glared out through the wickerwork with their yellow eyes.

"Huh!" Hide-Away laughed. "We've offended the two gentlemen. Never mind, it's all for their own good," and he bowed first to Mr Proud and then to Mr Ponder.

But when it came to Mr Percival's turn, Storm-Boy

couldn't bear to see him shut up too. Ever since the miracle of Mr Percival's rescue, he had been Storm-Boy's favourite. He was always quieter, more gentle, and more trusting than his two brothers. Storm-Boy picked him up, smoothed his wings, and held him close. "Poor Mr Percival," he said gently. He looked up at his father. "I'll hold Mr Percival," he said. "Can I, Dad?"

"Oh, all right," Hide-Away said, taking up the two baskets. "Come on, it's time we started."

Hide-Away sailed for five miles up the sanctuary before he stopped the boat.

"Here we are," he said at last.

Then he opened the two baskets and took out Mr Proud and Mr Ponder.

"Off you go," he said. "Now you'll have to look after yourselves." Then he pushed them off. They flew away in a high wide arc and made for the shore.

"Now Mr Percival," he said.

Storm-Boy pressed his head against Mr Percival's and gave his friend a last soft squeeze. "Good-bye, Mr Percival," he said. He had to pause for a second to clear his throat. "Be a . . . be a good pelican, Mr Percival, and look after yourself."

He lifted him over the side of the boat and put him down on the water as if he were a big rubber duck. Mr Percival looked surprised and pained for a minute and floated up and down on the ripples. Then he lifted his big wings, pedalled strongly, and rose slowly up over the water.

Storm-Boy brushed at his eye with his knuckles and looked away. He didn't want to let his father see his face.

HIDE-AWAY AND STORM-BOY spent the day fishing. It was fine and sunny, but somehow it seemed cold. Most of the time they just sat in the bobbing boat without talking, but Storm-Boy knew that his father knew what he was thinking. Sometimes Hide-Away looked at him strangely, and once he even cleared his throat carefully, gazed out across the water, and said in an unhappy gay voice: "Well, I wonder how the three Mr P's are feeling. As happy as Larry, I'll bet!" He looked rather miserably at Storm-Boy and went on with his fishing.

"Yes, I'll bet," Storm-Boy said, and also went on sadly with his fishing.

Towards evening they packed up and set off for home.

The sun was flinging a million golden mirrors in a lane across the water. It glowed on the bare patches of the sandhills and lit up the bushes and tussocks till every stem and twig shone with rosy fire. The little boat came gliding in to shore through the chuckle of the ripples.

Suddenly Storm-Boy looked up.

"Look, Dad! Look!" he shouted.

Hide-Away beached the boat and looked up to where Storm-Boy was pointing. "What?"

"Look! Look!" cried Storm-Boy.

High against the sky on the big sandhill stood the tall Look-Out Post that Hide-Away and Fingerbone had put up years before. And right on top of the post was a big shape. It was quite still, a statue on a column, a bird of stone.

Then, as if hearing Storm-Boy's startled voice, it suddenly spread out two big wings and launched itself into the air. As it banked against the western sun its beak and big black-tipped wings glowed in the shooting beams of light. For an instant it looked like a magic bird. Storm-Boy ran ahead, craning upwards, yelling and waving.

"Mr Percival! It's Mr Percival! Mr Percival has come back home!"

It was a happy reunion that night. Even Hide-Away seemed secretly glad that Mr Percival had come back.

"Yes, I suppose he can stay," he said; "as long as Mr Proud and Mr Ponder don't come back too. One pelican's appetite is bad enough; we can't cope with three."

And although Storm-Boy loved Mr Proud and Mr Ponder too, he found himself hoping very much that they would stay away.

And they did. As the days went by they sometimes swept overhead, or even landed on the beach for a while, but in the end they always returned to the sanctuary.

But not Mr Percival. He refused even to leave Storm-Boy's side.

WHEREVER STORM-BOY WENT, Mr Percival followed. If he collected shells along the beach, Mr Percival went with him, either waddling importantly along at his heels or flying slowly above him in wide circles. If Storm-Boy went swimming, or sliding down the sandhills, or playing on the sand, Mr Percival found a good spot near by and perched there heavily to watch and wait until it was over. If Storm-Boy went fishing or rowing on the Coorong, Mr Percival cruised joyously round him with his neck bent back and his chest thrust forward like a dragon-ship sailing calmly in a sea of air. Whenever he saw Storm-Boy anchor the boat he came gliding in with a long skimming splash, shook his wings into place, and bobbed serenely on the ripples a few yards away.

"Oh, you're a grand old gentleman, Mr Percival," Hide-Away said, laughing. "You ought to be wearing a top-hat, or maybe a back-to-front collar and a pair of spectacles. Then perhaps you could give the sermon or take the Sunday school lessons."

But Mr Percival merely held his head on one side and waited for Hide-Away to throw him a piece of fish—or two or three whole fish to pop into his creel.

Fingerbone and Hide-Away were both glad that Storm-Boy had found Mr Percival.

"Better than a watch-dog even," Fingerbone said. "Can't run much, but can *fly*."

"Can even chase after things like a dog," said Hide-Away. "You watch!"

It was true. They first learnt what a good catcher Mr Percival was when Storm-Boy was playing ball on the beach. It was a red and yellow ball that Hide-Away had brought back from Goolwa. Once when Storm-Boy threw it hard it went bouncing off toward Mr Percival.

"Look out!" Storm-Boy shouted.

But Mr Percival didn't look out. Instead he took two or three quick steps and snapped up the ball in his creel. Storm-Boy was horrified. He rushed up to Mr Percival, panting.

"You can't eat a *ball*," he yelled. "It's rubber, it's not a fish! Don't swallow it; you'll choke!"

Mr Percival listened to him very seriously for a minute, with his head held a bit more to one side than usual and his big beak parted in a sly smile. Then he stepped forward and dropped the ball at Storm-Boy's feet, just like a retriever.

After that, Storm-Boy often had fun on the beach with

Mr Percival. Whenever he threw the ball, or a smooth pebble, or a sea-urchin, or an old fishing reel, Mr Percival snapped it up and brought it back. Sometimes he threw things into the water. Mr Percival watched carefully with his bright eyes; then he flew out, landed on the right spot, and fished the prize out of the water. Then Storm-Boy would laugh and clap his hands and rub his fingers up and down the back of Mr Percival's neck. Mr Percival always liked this very much; the only thing he liked better was a good meal of fish.

One day as Hide-Away was watching them play he had an idea.

"If he can bring things back to you, perhaps he can carry things away too," he said. He gave Mr Percival a sinker and a bit of fishing line. "Now, take it to Storm-Boy," he said; "that's the fellow."

At first Mr Percival didn't understand, but at last, after many tries, he dropped the sinker at Storm-Boy's feet. Both Hide-Away and Storm-Boy clapped, and rubbed the back of Mr Percival's neck, and gave him a piece of fish. Mr Percival looked very pleased and proud.

After that Hide-Away asked Storm-Boy to stand out in the shallow water, and they played the game again. Before long Mr Percival could take a sinker and a small fishing line, fly out to Storm-Boy, and drop it beside him. But he always expected a piece of fish after each try.

They played the game for many weeks, sometimes with Storm-Boy in the water and sometimes with Hide-Away, until Mr Percival could carry a fishing line and drop it into the sea without any trouble. Then, when there was an off-shore wind from the north and the great seas flattened out sullenly, Hide-Away went far out from shore and Mr Percival practised carrying a long, long line to him.

"It's wonderful," Hide-Away said, laughing and clapping when he came back. "Now Mr Percival can help me with my fishing. He can carry out my mulloway lines for me." And he scratched Mr Percival's neck and gave him an extra piece of fish. "Mr Percival, you're as clever as a Chinese fishing bird," he said. And then he laughed, and so did Storm-Boy; and Mr Percival was so pleased with himself that he snickered and snackered happily for the rest of the day.

As time went by people began to talk about Storm-Boy and Mr Percival. Picnickers and Game Inspectors and passing fishermen saw them and began to spread the story.

"Follows him round like a dog," said old Sammy Scales in Goolwa. "Crazy, I tell you."

"I wouldn't have believed it," the postmaster said, "if I hadn't seen it with my own eyes."

And by and by many people did see it with their own eyes. For when Hide-Away and Storm-Boy set off on their trips to Goolwa, Mr Percival couldn't understand what was happening. He flew around and behind and ahead of them all the way, until they began to get near the town; then he landed and waited patiently on the river, until he saw the boat starting off for home again.

People used to hear about it and come to watch.

"Just like a dog," said Sammy Scales. "Crazy, I tell you. Some day the whole world will hear about this."

And then something happened that proved he was right.

It was the year of the great storms. They began in May, even before the winter had started. Shrieking and raging out of the south the Antarctic winds seemed to have lost themselves and come up howling in a frenzy to find the way.

In June they flattened the sedge, rooted out some of the bushes that had crouched on top of the sandhills for years, and blew out one of the iron sheets from the humpy. Hide-Away tied wires to the walls and weighed down the roof with driftwood and stones.

In July the winds lost their senses. Three great storms swept out of the south, the third one so terrible that it gathered up the sea in mountains, mashed it into foam, and hurled it against the shore. The waves came in like rolling railway embankments right up to the sandhills where Hide-Away and Storm-Boy lived. They lashed and tore at them as if they wanted to carry them away. The boobyalla bushes bent and broke. The humpy shivered and shook. Even Mr Percival had to go right inside or risk being blown away.

As night came on, Hide-Away battened up the doorway and spread extra clothing on the bunks.

"Better sleep now if you can," he said to Storm-Boy. "By morning the humpy might be blowing along on the other side of the Coorong."

In the darkness of early morning Storm-Boy suddenly woke with Hide-Away's voice in his ears.

"Quick, Storm-Boy," he said.

Storm-Boy jumped up. "Is the humpy blowing away?"

"No, it's a wreck!" Hide-Away said. "A shipwreck on the shore."

Storm-Boy put on two of his father's coats and followed him out to the top of the sandhill. Daybreak was coming like a milky stain in the east, but the world in front was just a white roar. Hide-Away put his mouth close to Storm-Boy's ear and pointed.

"Look!" he yelled. "Out there!"

Storm-Boy looked hard. There was a black shape in the

white. Fingerbone was standing on top of the sandhill holding on to the Look-Out Post.

"Tugboat," he shouted.

"Aground!" yelled Hide-Away.

Fingerbone nodded. "Storm too wild," he bellowed. "Poor fellows on tugboat . . ." He shook his head. "Poor fellows!"

When morning came over the world at last they could see the tugboat clearly, lying like a wounded whale, with huge waves leaping and crashing over it, throwing up white hands of spray in a devil-dance.

"They can never swim it or launch a boat," said Hide-Away. "Their only hope is a line to the shore."

"No one get line out," Fingerbone said. "Not today."

"No," said Hide-Away sadly. "And by tomorrow it will be too late." Sometimes in a lull between the waves they could see three or four men clinging to the tugboat, waving their hands for help.

"Look at them," Storm-Boy yelled. "We must help them! They'll be drowned."

"How can we help?" said his father. "We can't throw a line; it's too far."

"How far is it?"

"Too far. Two or three hundred yards at least."

"No blackfellow throw spear so far," said Fingerbone. "Not even half so far."

"Especially not with a line attached. We'd need a harpoon gun."

"Then I couldn't throw a stone a *quarter* of the way," Storm-Boy said. He picked up a pebble and hurled it towards the sea. It fell near the shore. "See," he said.

Suddenly there was a swish of big wings past them and Mr Percival sailed out over the spot where the pebble had fallen. He looked at the foam of the waves for a minute as if playing the old game of fetch-the-pebble-back; then he changed his mind, turned, and landed back on the beach.

Storm-Boy gave a great shout and ran towards him. "Mr Percival! Mr Percival is the one to do it! He can *fly*!"

Hide-Away saw what he meant. He raced back to the humpy and found two or three long fishing lines, as thin as thread. He tied them together and coiled them very carefully and lightly on a hard patch of clean sand. Then he took a light sinker, tied it to one end, and gave it to Mr Percival.

"Out to the ship," he said, pointing and flapping; "take it out to the ship."

Mr Percival looked puzzled and alarmed at the idea of fishing on such a wild day, but he beat his wings and rose up heavily over the sea.

"Out to the boat! Out to the boat!" they all shouted. But Mr Percival didn't understand. He flew too far to one side, dropped the line in the sea, and turned back.

"Missed," said Hide-Away, disappointed.

"But it was a good try," Storm-Boy said, as Mr Percival landed. He gave him a piece of fish and scratched his neck. "Good boy," he said. "Good boy, Mr Percival. In a minute we'll have another try."

But they missed again. This time Mr Percival flew straight towards the boat but didn't go out quite far enough. "Never mind," said Storm-Boy. "You're a good pelican for trying." He held Mr Percival like a big duck and gave him another piece of fish.

Again and again they tried, and again and again they missed. At first the men on the boat couldn't understand

46

what was going on, but they soon guessed, and watched every try hopefully and breathlessly.

Storm-Boy and Hide-Away were disappointed but they didn't give up. Neither did Mr Percival. He flew out and back, out and back, until at last, on the tenth try, he did it. A great gust of wind suddenly lifted him up and flung him sideways. He threw up his big wing and, just as he banked sharply over the tugboat, dropped the line. It fell right across the drowning ship.

"You've done it! You've done it!" Storm-Boy, Hide-Away, and Fingerbone shouted together as Mr Percival landed on the beach. "You're a good, brave, clever pelican." And they patted him, and fed him, and danced round him so much that poor Mr Percival couldn't quite understand what he'd done that was so wonderful. He kept snickering and snackering excitedly, opening his beak in a kind of grin, and eating more fish than he'd ever had before.

But the struggle to save the men on the tugboat was only just beginning. The captain seized the fishing line as it fell, waited for the next big wave to roll past, and then fastened the line to the end of a long coil of thin rope. Gently, very gently, he lowered it into the sea and waved to Hide-Away and Fingerbone to start pulling. They had to be very careful; if the line snagged, or if they pulled too sharply, the line might break and they would have to start all over again.

But they were lucky. At last the rope came lifting and flopping slowly out of the backwash. Fingerbone ran down to grab it. He danced and waved excitedly. Now the captain of the tug tied a heavy line to the thin rope, and the crew kept paying them out together, holding on desperately as the big waves and spray kept smashing over their ship.

Before long, Storm-Boy, Fingerbone, and Hide-Away

had hauled the end of the big rope ashore. Then they dragged it quickly up the sandhills to the Look-Out Post, where Hide-Away wound it firmly round and round the butt. Meanwhile the crew had fastened their end and had hitched a rough kind of bosun's chair to the rope. A man lashed himself in, and signalled to Hide-Away to start pulling on the thin rope. The rescue was ready to start.

The sea sprang and snatched at the man on the rope like a beast with white teeth. Sometimes, where the rope sagged lowest, the waves swept him right under. Storm-Boy could feel the shock and shudder of the line as the water thundered round it. But the man managed to snatch a breath between waves and he always rose up safely again on the rope. Hide-Away and Fingerbone pulled until their feet dug deep into the sand, and the muscles that stood out on their arms looked like the rope they were pulling. And so at last they were able to haul the man through the thud and tug of the sea to the shore, where he unfastened himself and dropped down on to the sand of the beach. He was shivering and exhausted, but he was safe. Storm-Boy ran down to help him up to the humpy.

Meanwhile the rest of the crew had hauled the rough bosun's chair back to the ship and another man was ready to be pulled ashore. After him came a third, who staggered feebly up the beach.

"Hurry," he said. "The boat's breaking up and there are still three men on board."

Hide-Away's forehead was wet, and Fingerbone puffed as they dug their feet in the sand and hauled.

"Hurry," they kept panting. "The boat's breaking up."

At last they had five men safely on shore and there was

48

only the captain to come. Then he, too, left the ship and they hauled again. He was a big man who weighed down the rope, and Hide-Away and Fingerbone were almost exhausted. Suddenly the rope grew taut, shuddered, and slackened.

"Quick," Hide-Away cried. "She's shifting."

Storm-Boy seized the pulling-rope and hauled.

"Hurry," yelled the captain. "She's going."

One or two of the crewmen who could still walk grabbed the line and helped to pull. Between them all they slowly hauled the captain ashore and dragged him, pale and half-drowned, on to the beach.

"Saved!" he kept saying weakly. "Saved by a miracle and a pelican."

Hide-Away and Storm-Boy kept the captain and his five crewmen in the humpy for a day. They gave them hot food and dried out their clothes. Next morning the storm began to clear and the sun flashed across the Coorong, so Hide-Away began preparing to sail the six of them up to Goolwa.

Before they left, the captain took Hide-Away aside.

"You saved our lives," he said, "you and your black friend, and especially the boy and the bird. We want to do something in return."

Hide-Away was embarrassed. "No need to worry about that," he said.

"But we've talked it over," said the captain, "and we've decided. We'd like to pay for the boy to go to school—to boarding school in Adelaide."

Hide-Away was sad. "He'd be very lonely, and so would I. His heart would be sick for the wind and the waves, and especially for Mr Percival."

"No matter," the captain said. "He's ten, or is it eleven?

Soon he'll be grown up, and yet he won't be able to read or write. It's not right to stop him."

Hide-Away hung his head. "Yes, you're right, he ought to go."

But when they called Storm-Boy and told him the captain's plan, he wouldn't go. "No!" he said horrified. "I won't leave Mr Percival! I won't!"

"But Storm-Boy."

"Not unless I'm allowed to take Mr Percival to school with me."

"You know you couldn't do that!"

"Then I won't go."

The captain shrugged. "Very well," he said to Hide-Away, "later perhaps. There'll always be a place ready for him." Then he said good-bye and scratched Mr Percival's neck. "You're a big, wonderful bird," he said. He looked up at Hide-Away. "When he dies you must send him to the museum; we'll put a label on the case: *The pelican that saved six men's lives.*"

Hide-Away looked round quickly. He was glad Storm-Boy hadn't heard the captain's words.

For the rest of the year everyone was happy. The storms went back to the cold south, the sun warmed the sandhills, and spring ran over the countryside with new leaves and little bush buds.

Before long the open season for duck-shooting came round again. All along the Coorong the shooters went, the blast of their guns echoing up and down the water, and the stench of their gunpowder hanging on the still air like a black fog of rotting smoke. The mornings were filled with the cries and screams of birds. Sometimes Storm-Boy could see the birds falling, or struggling westward, wounded and maimed, towards the shelter of the sanctuary.

From the start, Mr Percival hated the shooters. He

harried them whenever he could. Sometimes he just sat staring at them rudely until they grew impatient and chased him away. Sometimes he swam annoyingly near their hidden boats until they splashed or made a noise. But most of all he flew round and round their hiding places in wide circles like a cumbersome old aeroplane on patrol. And all of it was to help the ducks, to warn them in time, to keep them away from the shooters, so that the terrible guns would roar less often, and kill less often still.

Before long the ducks understood Mr Percival's warnings, and kept away. The shooters grew angrier and angrier.

"It's that confounded, pot-bellied old pelican again," they'd say. "He's worse than a seal in a fish-net."

"He's like a spy in the sky," said one. "We'll never shoot any ducks while he's about."

And so it went on until one terrible morning in February. Storm-Boy was standing high on the ridge of a sandhill watching the sun slip up from the sea like a blazing penny. He turned to look inland, and there behind a bending boobyalla bush near the Coorong he saw two shooters crouching. They were very still, waiting for six ducks out on the water to swim a little nearer. Just then Mr Percival came sweeping round in his ponderous flight. He swung in low over the hiding men, and the ducks gave a sudden cry of alarm, flapped strongly, and flew off very fast and low over the water.

The men shouted with rage. One of them leapt out, swung up his gun, and aimed at Mr Percival. Storm-Boy saw him and gave a great cry.

"Don't! Don't shoot! It's Mr Perc—"

His voice was drowned by the roar of the gun. Mr Percival seemed to shudder in flight as if he'd flown into a wall of glass. Then he started to fall heavily and awkwardly to the ground. Storm-Boy ran headlong towards the spot, tripping, falling over tussocks, stumbling into hollows, jumping up, racing, panting, crying out, his breath gulping in big sobs, his heart pumping wildly.

"Mr Percival! They've shot Mr Percival!" he kept screaming. "Mr Percival! Mr Percival!"

Poor Mr Percival! When Storm-Boy reached him he was trying to stand up and walk, but he fell forwards helplessly with one wing splayed out. Blood was moistening his white chest-feathers, and he was panting as if he'd just played a hard game.

"Mr Percival! Oh, Mr Percival!" It was all Storm-Boy could say. He kept on repeating it over and over again as he picked him up slowly and gently and then ran all the way back to the humpy.

Hide-Away was getting the breakfast when Storm-Boy burst in, sobbing.

"Mr Percival! They've shot Mr Percival!"

Hide-Away sprang round, startled, threw down the spoon he was using, and ran out to find the shooters. But they'd already gone. Ashamed and afraid, they'd quickly crossed to the other side of the Coorong, and driven off.

Hide-Away came back angrily. Then he took Mr Percival gently from Storm-Boy and examined him—wiped his chest and straightened the shattered feathers of his wing. Mr Percival snackered his beak weakly and panted rapidly.

"Will he . . . will Mr Percival . . . be all right?" Storm-Boy could hardly get the words out.

Hide-Away handed the wounded bird back to him silently and looked out through the doorway towards the far track where the shooters had disappeared. He couldn't bring himself to say anything.

All day long Storm-Boy held Mr Percival in his arms. In front of the rough iron stove where long ago he had first nursed the little bruised pelican into life, he now sat motionless and silent. Fingerbone tried to cheer him up, and Hide-Away offered him breakfast and dinner, but Storm-Boy shook his head and sat on, numb and silent. Now and then he smoothed the feathers where they were matted and stuck together, or straightened the useless wing. But in his heart he knew what was happening. Mr Percival's breathing was shallow and quick, his body and neck were drooping, and for long stretches at a time his eyes were shut. Then, suddenly, they would snap open again, clear and bright, and he would snacker his beak softly in a kind of sad, weak smile, before dozing off again.

"Mr Percival," Storm-Boy whispered, "you're the best, best friend I ever had."

Tea-time came, the sun dipped down, and long shadows began to move up from the hollows. For a while the tops of the high sandhills glowed golden in the evening light, but then they faded too and it was dark. Hide-Away didn't light the lantern. Instead, the three of them stayed on in front of the little fireplace—Hide-Away, Storm-Boy, and Mr Percival—while darkness filled the humpy and the stars came out as clear and pure as ice.

And at nine o'clock Mr Percival died.

Only then did Hide-Away move. He got up softly, and, gently, very gently, took Mr Percival from Storm-Boy. And Storm-Boy gave him up. Then at last he flung himself down on his bunk and sobbed softly to himself, hour after hour, until Hide-Away came over and put a hand on his shoulder.

"It's right that you should cry for Mr Percival for a while," he said, kindly and firmly; "but don't keep on brooding, Storm-Boy."

"B—But why did they shoot Mr . . . Mr Percival? He wasn—wasn't hurting anyone; jus—just warning the ducks like always."

"In the world," Hide-Away said sadly, "there will always be men who are cruel, just as there will always be men who are lazy or stupid or wise or kind. Today you've seen what cruel and stupid men can do."

He pulled a blanket over Storm-Boy and said quietly, "Now try to get some sleep."

But Storm-Boy didn't sleep. All night he lay clutching his cold wet pillow.

In the morning Hide-Away spoke to Storm-Boy.

"The sailors will arrange to have Mr Percival put in the museum," he said, "with a notice saying how he saved their lives—and how he lost his. Would you like that?"

Storm-Boy shook his head. "Mr Percival wouldn't have liked that," he said; "not to be shut up in a glass case for people to stare at. Never!"

And he took the spade and climbed to the top of the big sandhill by the Look-Out Post.

"Mr Percival would want to be buried here," he said, "by the foot of the Look-Out. This is his place for ever." And he began to dig.

Hide-Away nodded. Then he took a shovel and went up to dig too.

And so they buried Mr Percival deep beside the Look-Out Post on top of the golden sandhill, with the beach below, and the shining sand and the salt smack of the sea there day and night—and all around was the wide sky, and the tang of the open air, and the wild lonely wind in the scrub.

When they'd finished, Storm-Boy stood for a long time looking silently all around him. Then he turned to Hide-Away.

"All right," he said, "I'm ready to go now if you like."

"Go? Where to?"

"To school! Like the sailors said."

"Oh! Oh, yes . . . Very well, then."

Hide-Away knew then that without Mr Percival Storm-Boy wouldn't be able to live there; at least not for a while.

Together they walked slowly down the sandhill to the humpy.

"We'll leave the boat in Goolwa for a few days," Hide-Away said. "I'll have to go up to Adelaide with you to get you settled in."

And that was how Storm-Boy went to school. Hide-Away came back to the humpy by the Coorong to start the long, long wait for the school holidays. You can see him there now. By day, Fingerbone sometimes comes to talk to him, but at night he stands alone beside the Look-Out Post and gazes out at the sea and the clouds of the western storms; and, a hundred miles away in Adelaide, Storm-Boy sits by the boarding-school window and looks out at the tossing trees and the windy sky.

And everything lives on in their hearts—the wind-talk and wave-talk, and the scribblings on the sand; the Coorong, the salt smell of the beach, the humpy, and the long days of their happiness together. And always, above them, in their mind's eye, they can see the shape of two big wings in the storm-clouds and the flying scud—two wings of white with trailing black edges—spread across the sky.

For birds like Mr Percival do not really die.